# DR XARGLE'S BOOK OF EARTH TIGGERS

Translated into Human by Jeanne Willis
Pictures by Tony Ross

Ⓐ

Andersen Press · London

Good morning, class.

Today we are going to learn about Earth Tiggers.
Earth Tiggers are made of furry material. This does
up underneath with pink buttons.

They are available in Patterned or Plain.

Press them in the middle to find the squeaker.

Earth Tiggers grow sharp thorns.
These they use to carve objects made of wood.

Or to climb steep Earthlets.

Earth Tiggers like gardening. They dig a hole and
plant a stinkpod. This never grows.

During the rainy season, stinkpods may be planted
in any container found in the earthdwelling.

Earth Tiggers like breakfast at 5 a.m. Precisely.
They massage the pyjamas of the sleeping Earthlet.
Then they sit on his nostrils.

Earth Tiggers eat meatblob.

This they collect on their many antennae to save for later.

A healthy Earth Tigger also needs cowjuice, tandoori cluck bird, muckworm and old green gibble in dustbin gravy.

Earth Tiggers can hear a parcel of pigrolls being opened five earth miles away.

They cannot hear an Earthlet shouting "Tiddles!" in the next garden.

Earth Tiggers hate the Earth Hound.
They fold in half and puff air into their waggler.
Then they go into orbit with a hiss and a crackle.

In a glass capsule full of stones and vegetables lives
the sparkly, golden fishstick.

This the Earth Tigger likes. He puts his mitten into the water and mixes the fishstick all about.

Earth Tiggers like to sing loudly in the moonlight with their friends. The Earthling hurls items of footwear all around.

Earth Tiggers sometimes put a hairy pudding on the stairs. The Earthling is made to step on this with no socks on.

Repeat this phrase after me:
"Whoops, I have slipped on a furball and broken both my legs."

Sometimes the Earth Tigger gets torn and must be taken to the menders. First he must be caught and wrapped in cardboard and string. The Earthlet sticks himself back together with pink paper.

When Earth Tiggers are born, the Earthlet gives them a bed made from knitted twigs and a bag of birdfluff. This the Tiggerlets hate.

They go to sleep in the headdress of the Earthling.

Dear me, is that the time?
Put on your disguises and get into the spaceship quickly.
We're going to Planet Earth to stroke Tiggerlets.

We'll be landing in India at dinnertime.